T0208067

ALPHA SPIES

WRONG TIMING

CHARITY TEH

For book orders, email orders@traffordpublishing.com.sg

Most Trafford Singapore titles are also available at major online book retailers.

Printed in Singapore.

ISBN: 978-1-4669-2824-4 (sc)
ISBN: 978-1-4669-2825-1 (hc)
ISBN: 978-1-4669-2826-8 (e)

Trafford rev. 11/09/2012

www.traffordpublishing.com.sg

Singapore
toll-free: 800 101 2656 (Singapore)
Fax: 800 101 2656 (Singapore)

Chapter 1

Vickie was exhausted. Her parents had sent her and Kyle to their aunt's farm for the whole summer vacation. Vickie reeked of manure and was nearly burned by the heat.

Finally their aunt called them in for some lemonade. Kyle was inside in a blink of an eye but Vickie was too exhausted too move. She trudged inside and poured out the golden liquid into a glass, carrying it up to her bedroom. Kyle was waiting for her with a jar of cookies.

"I've cleaned out the hens' cage and swept up the leaves in the back yard," Kyle grinned. "What did you do?"

Vickie was
exhausted.

Vickie sighed. She still couldn't believe the fact that Kyle actually *enjoyed* the vacation.

"I fed the ponies in the stable," Vickie replied. She dropped her voice to a hushed whisper. "Is the locket safe?"

Kyle nodded and pulled open a drawer. A few weeks ago, they had been recruited by the Alpha Spies to defeat someone called Oceanus and find a magical locket. Vickie took the locket and opened it smiling.

Suddenly, a small piece of paper with writing fell out of the locket. Vickie picked it up as it fell on the pillow and read it carefully.

Found another villain. Must meet to discuss. Go to local library, classics section. Bring iPad and UV light and any other gadgets if necessary.

-> Minerva

"Wow." Kyle exclaimed. "*Another* mission!"

"Awesome." Vickie leapt up and down on the bed, only to accidentally trip over Kyle's foot and land flat on her face.

Kyle laughed. He grabbed his iPad and raced for the door. Vickie followed excitedly, pocketing her ultraviolet light/plasma gun. Vickie was just in time to fasten the clasp of the magical locket before they scurried down the stairs. They grabbed a chocolate bar each, got their bikes out of the shed, dived between a flock of geese and then rode off to the library.

When they arrived, Minerva was already waiting for them with a large file. They sat down at a table and looked at the papers and documents.

"Apparently, our villain is in the Victorian era." Minerva said. "He's messing up time and causing the years to adjust differently, so that the Alpha Spies wouldn't have existed."

"Okay . . ." Vickie looked at the documents, then at Minerva. "How are we going to get in the Victorian era?"

"The Alpha Spies have a time machine." Minerva replied. "We'll travel back in time, try to stop the villain and get back before anyone other than the Alpha Spies finds out."

"Cool!" Kyle's smile reached his ears. "But where's Janie, and the others?"

"They're doing research on the villains," Minerva answered. "Same goes for me, this time you'll have to survive on your own."

"Cool." Kyle leapt to his feet in excitement. Suddenly Vickie's phone rang. She answered it and heard Reuben's voice on the other end.

"Is the locket safe?" Reuben asked through the phone.

"Yes. We got our mission data already." Vickie said.

"We have got our time machine ready and charged with battery juice. Come to the headquarters immediately and try to avoid Ginger. She's been acting weird lately."

"We'll try." Vickie laughed and turned off her phone. "We have to get to the headquarters."

"The headquarters are underwater." Kyle remembered. "I just don't know which part of the ocean it is in."

"It is in another dimension." Minerva stood up. She held up a tube.

"I've seen that!" Kyle grinned and stepped into the tube with Vickie.

Everything went black.

Chapter 2

"Ouch."

They had landed on a clump of seaweed and there wasn't much of it. They looked around cautiously and recalled the last time they came here.

The food vault was still there, that was good. So were the spy jackets.

Kyle was climbing into the food vault grinning. Vickie sighed and followed.

"You'd better not drink any more Cokes." Vickie reasoned. "We don't want you to be poisoned again."

"Good point." Kyle grabbed a plate of spaghetti and a fork. He began to shovel them in his mouth as Vickie opened a book on the Victorians.

"We need to get some Victorian clothes if we want to blend in," Vickie said. She slammed her book shut, making Kyle jump and nearly spill his spaghetti.

"Hey, what was that for?"

"We need to find some Victorian outfits." Vickie repeated. She opened a drawer that was labeled 'PAINT' and smeared some of the black paint on Kyle's face. "There were a lot of poor people in Victorian times. Now you look like one."

Kyle scowled. He polished off his spaghetti and climbed back up to the main HQ hall. He glanced around and saw Ginger staring at him.

Kyle glared at Ginger. A microchip had been implanted into Kyle's brain to hear what Ginger (the cat) was thinking. Ever since Ginger found out, she'd been bugging him ever since.

We meet again, humanoid. This time, cats will win. Your puny weapons will not destroy us. We . . . will . . . rule . . .

Ginger hissed angrily and climbed on a couch. Minerva and Reuben were there waiting for them laughing.

She slammed her book shut, making
Kyle jump and nearly spill his spaghetti.

"Where is this time machine anyway?" Kyle asked, trying to ignore Ginger's voice in his brain.

"Just through that door." Reuben replied. He opened a door and Vickie and Kyle gasped.

There were glass pods around the room and scientific equipment on tables. They turned around but Reuben wasn't there anymore. They tried the door but it was locked.

Kyle stamped his foot on the ground. "We're going to die of boredom! What could be worse?" He banged his head on the wall in frustration.

But Vickie was too fascinated by the last giant pod in the middle of the room. As if in a trance, she walked slowly to it Kyle ran to her, but it was too late.

Vickie disappeared with a misty puff of smoke leaving Kyle alone in the room. Kyle smashed his fist against the glass, only to be sucked in as well.

There was a misty grey blur around him. He couldn't see much, but he knew he and Vickie were in BIG trouble.

Chapter 3

The noise and bustle of the marketplace was deafening. Vickie looked around her. Someone shoved a basket of carrots into her face and Vickie sighed. They must already be in the Victorian era.

Wait, who was 'They'?

"Kyle?" She whipped her head around frantically but there was no Kyle. She stamped her foot and ran off into the crowd.

This was what had happened to Kyle.

He had got out of the portal a few minutes before Vickie. He strolled down the streets and past the shops. He was stopped by a boy about his age. The boy had brown hair and green eyes.

"What're you doing in my territory?" the boy yelled at him. Kyle backed away slowly.

"Sorry, I didn't mean to." Kyle stammered.

"You'd better. I'm Thomas Silver, but you can call me Tom."

"Um—I'm Kyle."

"So . . ." Tom sat down next to a garbage can. "Since when are posh kids like you not in school?"

"Err—I don't go to school . . ."

"So you're a street kid like me, eh?"

"Um-" Kyle nodded.

"Say, where'd you get those shoes?" Tom pointed to Kyle's Nike trainers.

Kyle froze. "Err—I got them from a very rich and distant uncle . . ."

Tom smiled. Then he turned to the hut behind him. "That's where I live. You should come sometimes."

"I'm Thomas Silver, but you can call me Tom."

Kyle grinned nervously. "Thanks." He ran off into the crowd.

Meanwhile, Vickie was checking every inch of the square for signs of Kyle. A stray dog padded up to her excitedly and she petted it, happy to have company.

"Hey, little guy." She whispered to the dog. "Can you help me find my brother?" She took out Kyle's old handkerchief from her pocket and the dog sniffed it. It took off and Vickie ran after it.

The dog stopped at a shop and Vickie walked inside hopefully. Kyle was in there looking at some really old toys.

"Kyle!"

Kyle turned and his face broke into a smile of joy. "Vickie!"

"Where have you been? I had to use this dog to track you and-"

"Never mind about that." Kyle muttered. "We've got a mission which must not be delayed!" He said the last sentence with a dignified look.

Vickie grinned. "Let's go!"

Chapter 4

Vickie checked her phone for the billionth time. No new messages.

What a good agency, she thought sarcastically. *They send us on a mission without any data about the villain.*

That's when her phone rang. She whipped her phone back out of her pocket and answered it. She didn't recognize this number but she was happy to have someone to talk to other than Kyle.

"Hi, this is Calyx. Is this Vickie answering?"

"Yes." Vickie wondered who Calyx was and why she wanted her.

"I'm from Alpha Spies. Are you in the Victorian era yet?"

"Yes."

"Good. You need to track down Kronos. Just like Oceanus in your previous mission, he is part of an organization dedicated to Greek mythology. Not that they're the real gods, of course."

Vickie smiled. "Thanks for the info, Calyx." She hung up and Kyle stared at her questioningly. "Who's Calyx?" he asked.

"She's an agent from the Alpha Spies." Vickie replied. She told Kyle about Kronos with Kyle interrupting every ten seconds.

"So we have to track him down?" Kyle exclaimed. "We have to search every single bit of the world?"

"Of course not, dweeb. Why do you think the Alpha Spies sent us to Victorian Britain for?" She looked at a nearby sign. "Victorian Manchester, I guess."

The dog was still next to Vickie. She patted it and looked at Kyle. "We can't just abandon it, you know."

Kyle nodded in agreement. "We should use it as a watchdog. I'm naming it!"

Vickie rolled her eyes. Kyle loved to name things. "Yeah, whatever."

Kyle thought for a bit. "I'm going to call the dog . . . Zubin."

"Zubin? What kind of a name is that for a dog?"

"A weird one." Kyle grinned.

Zubin wagged his tail happily. He got up and began to lick Kyle. Kyle pushed him off and stood up.

"We need to find someone that knows a lot about what happens in this city." Vickie said.

"Don't worry." Kyle reassured. "I know exactly who to ask."

. . . .

A few minutes later, they arrived puffing and panting at Tom's hut.

"Nobody told me that it was uphill all the way." Kyle groaned. Vickie rang the doorbell but there was no answer. She pushed the door open nervously. The

Zubin wagged his tail happily.

creak of the door was deafening but there was still no sound.

Kyle went inside. "Maybe they're out shopping and left the door open."

"I don't think so." Vickie said. "The kettle's still boiling. Not many people leave the kettle on when they go out to buy things."

Kyle looked into the next room and widened his eyes in dismay. Vickie went over to him and gasped. There, in front of them was Tom, bound and gagged and thrown into a corner.

Tom raised his eyebrows and tried to speak but the cloth over his mouth muffled the sound, making it indecipherable. They ran to him and pulled out the cloth. Tom coughed and spluttered for a while, then glanced up at them. "Thanks."

"What happened to you?" Kyle demanded.

"Well," Tom shuddered. "I was helping my mum make tea, and suddenly this monster came into the kitchen. It tied me up and threw me in here."

"Do you remember anything else?" Vickie asked.

Tom closed his eyes and tried to remember. He opened his eyes again and smiled. "He had a scar in the shape of a K on his torso."

Vickie and Kyle looked at each other. "Kronos." they said instantaneously.

"Kro-what?" Tom looked confused.

Vickie turned back to Tom. "Well I guess we have to tell you everything now." She poured out the whole story.

"Spy time travelers." Tom said. "That is awesome."

Kyle nodded. He looked behind him. A trail of muddy hooves was behind him. "Kronos is a horse?"

Vickie laughed. "Possibly."

Tom grinned. "Let's go find Kronos."

Chapter 5

Calyx Kohen stepped out of the portal. Fortunately, nobody noticed her amid the crowd. She was afraid that the light from the time portal would draw people for a closer look.

The time portal disappeared. She let out a gasp of relief. Now, nobody would wonder what was going on.

That was when she realized the clothes she was wearing wasn't actually Victorian. She was also a teenager, and teenagers in the Victorian times didn't exactly wear jeans.

She broke into a run and hid in a dark corner of the marketplace. She dialed Vickie's number and waited.

Calyx Kohen stepped out of the portal.

A few seconds later Vickie answered the phone. "Where are you?" Calyx asked.

"We're at the train station." Vickie replied. "Meet us there."

Calyx hung up and glanced around. She could see smoke rising from a distant building. That must be the train station, she thought to herself. She headed for where the smoke was and saw Vickie and Kyle waiting for them.

Vickie smiled and waved. Calyx laughed. "How did you know that was me?" she asked.

Kyle rolled his eyes. "It's easy to spot someone from the future if they're wearing jeans and a bright pink backpack."

Calyx nodded in agreement, and then noticed the other member of their team. "Um, who are you?"

The boy grinned. "I'm Tom."

Vickie explained. "He was attacked by Kronos."

Kyle patted the dog fondly. "And this is Zubin," he said. "The best dog ever!"

Zubin's ears twitched at the sound of his name.

Calyx unzipped her backpack and pulled out a laptop. Tom's eyes widened.

"What's with all the fancy buttons?" he pointed at the keyboard.

Calyx giggled. "It's to make the laptop work. For instance, this is how you turn it on . . ."

Vickie and Kyle guffawed with laughter. Tom stared at Calyx. "Wow. This must be very expensive."

Calyx shrugged. "No, it was only about 360 dollars."

Tom yelled. *"It was 360 dollars? You actually have that much money?"*

Calyx cocked her head to one side. "You really *are* a Victorian aren't you?"

Kyle laughed. "Don't worry, Tom. All thanks to inflation, people of the future have a lot more money."

He waited for a response from Tom but Tom's eyes were fixed to something behind him. He whirled around and saw an evil-looking satyr about 7 feet tall.

"K-k-kronos . . ." Tom stammered. Kronos grinned evilly and pulled something out of thin air. Green gas wafted out and they began to feel nauseous. They dropped onto the hard ground and blacked out.

Chapter 6

A few minutes later, Kyle woke up in a dark cell. Dazed, he looked around him and saw Tom and Zubin next to him. Vickie and Calyx were chained up in a corner of the room.

"If Kronos comes to interrogate us," Calyx said. "Don't tell him anything. He'll get mad at you and I'll pick the lock without him looking."

Tom and Kyle nodded simultaneously. Hearing footsteps, they got into position and Kronos opened the cell door.

"Tell me," he said, with a hint of anger in his voice, "What are you doing in the Victorian era hunting me down?"

"What are you doing in the Victorian era hunting me down?"

Kyle shook his head. "Do you think we're stupid? We're not the type of people who listen to goats." He looked across to Calyx, who had finished picking her lock and moving on to Vickie's. She winked.

Tom stuck out his tongue at Kronos. That was a bad move. Kronos started to turn blood red and bellowed at Tom and Kyle, sending a huge sound wave rippling through the air. Zubin whined and Kronos kicked him. Zubin hit the wall and lay flat on the floor.

Calyx finished picking the locks and jumped on Kronos' back to create a diversion. Tom picked up Zubin and ran with Kyle to the open entrance. Vickie followed and Calyx leapt off, did a perfect cartwheel and stood back up when she was out of the cell. She shut the door and it locked with a satisfying click.

"Great." Tom grinned. "But what do we do now?"

Kyle looked at Kronos. "He will *escape* in a few minutes. That was just buying us some time."

Calyx agreed. They darted outside and Calyx began to phone HQ. Reuben answered with a gasp of relief.

"Phew. We thought Kronos had captured you!" Reuben laughed.

"He did." Calyx said. She explained what had happened.

"We need you to come back to 2012." Reuben replied. "We'll put a time portal where you are in a minute."

Calyx hung up. Soon, the portal's glimmering light appeared in front of them. One by one, they jumped through into a milky white universe.

They sat on the couch with a mug of hot chocolate each as Minerva and Reuben explained.

"We've hacked into Kronos' archives and it says," Reuben said. "It says that after he goes to the Victorian era, he will go to his organization's HQ."

"So we have to look for it, and then bring back a report?" Calyx asked.

Reuben nodded. "You should leave Zubin here. In 2112, the RSPCA might not exist anymore."

"The RSPCA won't exist anymore?" Kyle yelled.

"It's just a theory." Minerva smiled. "But it should be safe enough to bring Zubin along."

"What's the RSPCA?" Tom demanded.

Nobody heard him. They were too busy creating a time portal. They dived through and waited for 2112 to arrive.

Chapter 7

They landed on solid pavement and looked around them. They were in the middle of a grassy field. They waded through the thick grass and found themselves in the large, bustling city of 2112.

"Great." Calyx said. "Now what do we do?"

Kyle thought a bit. "We should get some hover boards!" he concluded. "I always wanted one."

Vickie shrugged. "No harm getting one, I guess."

They walked inside a shop and stood at the counter. "We want some hover boards, please."

The sales clerk laughed. "Do you think this is an antique shop or something?"

"Um—no, but-"

"Hover boards became out of fashion 15 years ago. Now," she pulled out a purple tube. "We use teleporters."

"Oh." Calyx grinned. "I guess we should have known that." She pulled out the teleporter they used to get to HQ.

"Now you're on the right track!" The sales clerk smiled. "You're not from around here, are you?"

"No." Tom clarified. "We're not."

"Just take it." The sales clerk pushed the teleporter across the counter. "You never know when you might need it."

"Thanks." Vickie shoved the teleporter into her pocket and they went outside.

Kyle sighed. "Great, so we're in 2112 and we have a teleporter. But we still have no idea where Kronos is."

"I think this may help." Calyx turned on her laptop and a bubble popped up on the screen.

Calyx turned on her laptop and a bubble popped up on the screen.

WELCOME TO 2112

"It *knows* what year we're in?" Kyle exclaimed. "Don't you have to adjust the time on the computer first?"

Calyx shook her head. She clicked on a program at the corner of the desktop screen and a giant map appeared on the screen.

She typed the word 'Kronos' into a box and a tiny red dot started blinking. The map zoomed itself to a blurry scene, then sharpened. Kronos was entering an elevator, scrolling through his inbox on his phone. He wasn't a satyr anymore, but the two gold horns on the back of his head proved his identity.

Calyx copied the code of the location into her USB device and stuck it into a hole in the teleporter. The teleporter flashed yellow once, twice, three times, and it turned into a giant portal. Tom retreated slowly. "Is this supposed to be normal in your time?"

"No." Vickie answered. "Well, not with most people."

"I guess we'd better go then." Kyle said. He climbed in the portal and vanished. The others followed and materialized later in front of the same titanium building that Kronos had been at a minute ago.

"I suppose we have to go in there." Calyx said. She headed for the elevator button, only to be zapped by a high-security laser. She stepped back, rubbing her arm in pain.

Kyle chuckled. "One thing you should know if you're a secret agent," he pointed to the panel next to the doorway. "Everything clandestine has a password."

Calyx groaned. "We'd better get cracking then."

Chapter 8

One bad thing about high technology was that they took so long to disable. Sweat beaded from Calyx's forehead as she cut the last wire in the panel, shutting down all the security systems in the building.

They entered the elevator and scanned all the floor buttons. "Where to now?" Kyle asked.

Vickie shrugged. Then she noticed a small bump on the floor. She knelt down and touched it gently. It was actually a trapdoor leading down to a stairway.

"I think Kronos went down here!" she yelled to the others. She started climbing down the steps and Kyle followed eagerly. The others did the same and Zubin padded along next to Calyx. She patted him fondly.

After what seemed like forever, they came to a halt at an iron vent. They heard people talking and they peered down into the room below them. They recognized Kronos, who was sitting on a wooden chair, arms folded. Oceanus, their former enemy, was next to him wearing a smug look on his face. There were other people there, some human, some animal and some a mixture of both. But there was one being different from all of them.

At the front of the room, there stood a cloaked figure. Nobody had ever seen his face, and he wore black gloves and a black coat. Kyle shivered. He dreaded the thought of what could be under those dark garments.

The mystery person began to speak. "Why have you not succeeded in your missions?" His voice had a hint of a Russian accent to it.

A person in the back row spoke up. "It's not that easy, master. Ever since you started being addicted to cigarettes, we don't have enough money to pay for food."

"Silence, you zombie scum!" The cloaked figure bellowed. Light ricocheted from his staff and struck the person in the chest. Soon, all that was left of him was ashes. The audience shrunk back uneasily.

"Fine. I will double your payment," he began with a glint in his eye, "But the person who manages to bring back the heads of Kyle, Vickie and Calyx, will get five times more money than anyone else!"

Kyle flinched at the sound of his name and stepped back instinctively. Unfortunately, his right foot accidentally cracked an old twig in half, causing the cloaked figure to look up at the vent. A wicked grin emerged from his face. "Get them!"

"Come on!" Vickie ran, Zubin scurrying along at her heels. Kyle and Tom followed them, Calyx trailing from behind. Calyx pulled out a pistol from her

"Silence, you zombie scum!"

belt and started firing at the trolls, goblins and other assorted mythological creatures that were swarming after them.

They emerged into the sunlight and ran for their lives. Vickie tossed her plasma gun to Calyx and Calyx mumbled a quick but grateful thanks. The creatures were appearing as fast as they fell dead.

Then Kyle remembered. "Vickie! The locket!"

Kyle's voice was nearly inaudible, muffled by the deafening sound of the troll's blood spattering all over the floor, but Vickie understood, nodding in confirmation. She grabbed the locket and yelled at the top of her voice:

"I wish that all the creatures would disappear!"

Her moment of heroism ended as nothing happened. The same old bullets kept firing, the same old trolls kept dying. She slapped her forehead in disbelief. *Of course,* she thought. *The locket could only do one at a time.*

She sighed. She had to do it the hard way after all.

Chapter 9

"I wish for that troll to disappear!"

"I wish for another one to disappear too!"

"Another one!"

"And another one!"

Her repeated cry was answered swiftly, the trolls vanishing into thin air like magic. *Well*, she thought to herself. *It was magic.*

Soon after, all the trolls had disappeared, along with the bloodstains they made with their open wounds.

Vickie collapsed, the weight of her magic forcing her to bend with tiredness. The locket started to burn, as the magic was too much for the locket. The clasp had broken off completely from Vickie's neck

"I wish for that troll to disappear!"

and Tom picked up the burning pendant and dunked it into a nearby puddle. The flame died out slowly, the smoke wafting into the air silently as a farewell tribute to the locket.

Calyx and Kyle helped the shaken body of Vickie up and Vickie began to cough and splutter. "The locket's broken." She said. "How are we ever going to tell Minerva?"

"Well, it *was* her great-great-great grandma's," Calyx reasoned, "But I think it would be the right thing to tell her."

Tom nodded. "Even though I haven't a clue what you're yakking on about, I can tell by Calyx's voice that you should tell whoever Minerva is."

Kyle laughed. "You seem to be catching on with our 'futuristic' slang terms."

Tom laughed too. "Yakking? Oh, please."

Suddenly, Vickie's phone rang with the usual Pink Panther tone she always used. Zubin began barking suspiciously. Being a Victorian dog, he wasn't used to all these techno stuff. Tom raised his eyebrows. "What is that?"

"It's a phone." Kyle explained, with a hint of humour in his voice. He knew where this was going.

"What's a phone?"

Calyx began to guffaw. "A phone is a device used to communicate around the world without means of transportation."

Tom knew none the better. "Um . . . is that something to eat?"

Calyx took a deep breath. "Okay, to explain it in easier terms, you can use it to talk to someone if that person is in a different place as you."

"Hmm. That's nice." Tom grinned halfheartedly and watched Vickie as she hung up her call.

"It's Reuben." She said. "They're going to open a portal in an hour so we'd better buy souvenirs or something." She smiled. "Especially Tom. It's not everyday you get pulled into a time-travel mission."

So they went off into the busy streets of 2112 again, pausing at the shops to see if they could get anything they wanted. Kyle wanted to get another teleporter but Vickie shook her head. "What's the point when you can use them any old time you want in 2012?"

So after about half an hour of searching, Vickie decided on an invisibility glove, Calyx a high-tech phone with infinite data and Kyle a translation device that he stuck in his ear. Now he would have no problem with his Spanish lessons.

All Tom wanted was a coin. "Why on Earth do you want a coin for, Tom?" Calyx asked feeling surprised. "All it's worth in your time is a lump of metal with a head on it."

"Well, it's got a year on it." Tom retorted back. "Plus, I don't want riches. All I want is the memory."

Kyle punched him on the shoulder lightly. "We really are going to miss you when you go back to your time."

Tom punched him back. "Me too."

That was when the portal flashed open in front of them. The hurried voice of Reuben rang out through the light: "Come on, get in before it closes!"

They got in and the whiteness enclosed them again.

Chapter 10

Tom Silver was going to go back.

It was time for him to go, and Kyle, Calyx and Vickie were waving sullenly. A tear slipped from Kyle's eye. He was going to miss him a lot.

Clutching the coin from 2112 in his fist tightly, Tom waved with his other hand. Zubin began to bark again. He didn't know what the fuss was all about and began to wonder why Tom was standing on the other side of a glowing hoop.

"I'm really going to miss you." Tom said, fighting back sobs.

"Well, you've got a coin to remember us by," Calyx replied comfortingly.

"I don't need a coin to remember you by." Tom smiled. "No-one could ever forget you."

Then the portal closed, leaving them in a deathly silence.

Vickie and Kyle's summer holiday had come to an end. They walked down the dusty path and talked about their mission.

"I think I've seen Tom somewhere before, but I can't place how." Vickie wondered out loud.

"I think so too," Kyle replied.

Suddenly, a voice came out from behind them. "Hey Kyle! Hey Vickie! How was your holiday?"

They turned and saw their friend Ash behind them. "Well, it was . . . interesting." Vickie smiled pleasantly.

But Kyle thought something that Vickie didn't. "Say, Ash, what's your full name?"

Ash grinned. "It's Ash Silver. My name is Ash Thomas Silver."

And glittering on a gold chain fastened on his neck, was a coin dated 2112.

And glittering on a gold chain fastened on his neck, was a coin dated 2112.

Printed in the United States
By Bookmasters